FOR MY WIFE, NORMA, WHO BELIEVED IN ME

NORMAN BRIDWELL'S
Clifford
COLLECTION

SCHOLASTIC INC.

New York   Toronto   London   Auckland
Sydney   Mexico City   New Delhi   Hong Kong

SPECIAL THANKS TO:

✳ The McCain Library and Archives at the University of Southern Mississippi for providing "Pencil trace from the cover of *Clifford the Big Red Dog*, Circa 1963."

✳ The Howard County Memory Project (sponsored by the Kokomo-Howard County Public Library) for providing the childhood photo of Norman Bridwell.

✳ Victoria Keyser for providing "A painting Norman sent in response to his first piece of fan mail, Circa 1963."

TABLE OF CONTENTS

DEAR READER,

Clifford has been a big part of my life for fifty years now, and I am so pleased to be able to share him with you in this collection of classic Clifford stories.

When I was a child, I spent much of my free time drawing imaginary people in imaginary scenes. I remember walking to and from school making up these stories. At the end of the day, I'd illustrate them on scrap paper my father had brought home from work for me.

After I finished high school, I dreamed of doing cartoon-style illustrations for magazines and newspapers. My mother suggested that I go to art school, and I took her advice. While I was there, I found that people enjoyed my **FUNNY ILLUSTRATIONS** and stories filled with wordplay.

IN 1962, my wife thought I should try to illustrate children's books. I showed my paintings to several publishers, but no one was interested. I was very disappointed, but there was a ray of hope! One editor told me to try writing a story based on my painting of a little girl with a very big dog. I was so excited that I wrote the story in just three days.

When my story was bought by Scholastic and published in 1963, I was shocked! I had not expected **CLIFFORD THE BIG RED DOG** to be published. Thanks to Scholastic, and some very wonderful editors, the Clifford books were born . . . and my life changed completely.

Because of Clifford, I have traveled all over the world. The Clifford books themselves have taken quite a journey, too. They've **DELIGHTED CHILDREN** as far away as Siberia. I know because I've gotten letters from children who live there.

Creating Clifford has also given me the opportunity to meet incredible people like the President and First Lady of the United States, movie actors, newspeople, and famous authors and artists that I admire.

But most wonderful of all, Clifford has brought me into the lives of many children. **I AM VERY LUCKY.** I love kids, and I love to make them laugh – and I hope whether you're a kid or a grown-up, that's just what this classic collection will make you do.

Sincerely,
Norman Bridwell

WHO IS NORMAN

Norman Bridwell, Circa 1936

On February 15, 1928, the Bridwell family welcomed their second son, Norman, into the world.

As a child in Kokomo, Indiana, Norman always liked to draw. "But I was never considered very good," says Norman. "In school there was always someone better than me; the art teacher always liked their work better than mine." But that didn't stop Norman from following his dream of becoming an artist. After high school, Norman went to art school and then moved to New York City.

BRIDWELL?

In 1962, Norman decided to show his drawings to several children's book publishers. He hoped that one of them might need a new illustrator. Norman was turned away from all of them, but one editor gave him some advice. While looking at Norman's painting of a little girl and a horse-size bloodhound, she said, "Why not try writing a story to go along with this picture?"

Original Clifford painting, 1962

" WRITE ABOUT what makes you FEEL GOOD. "

MEET THE REAL EMILY ELIZABETH

In just a few short days, Norman excitedly wrote a story about a little girl and her very big dog.

"I wanted to call the dog 'Tiny,' but Norma [his wife] said that was boring and suggested 'Clifford' after an imaginary friend from her childhood," Norman says. Deciding on the little girl's name, however, was easy. Norman named her Emily Elizabeth, after his young daughter.

"Having a character named after her was no big thing to Emily Elizabeth until she was grown up," says Norman. "But when she went to get her first library card one of the librarians asked, 'Are you

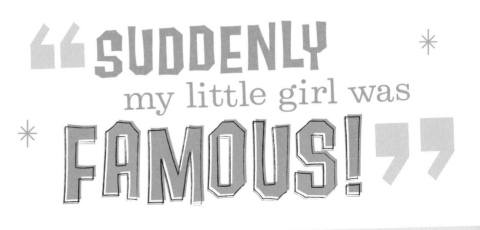

Norman and Emily Elizabeth, Circa 1964

the real Emily Elizabeth?' Emily Elizabeth was a bit confused. It never really sank in that she was known all over the country."

"SUDDENLY my little girl was FAMOUS!"

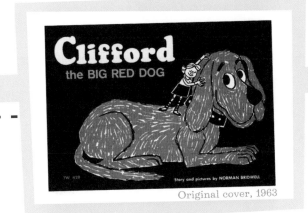
Original cover, 1963

CLIFFORD IS A
SUCCESS!

When ***Clifford the Big Red Dog*** was originally published by Scholastic in 1963, Norman told his wife, "Don't count on there being any more books."

But it was no fluke. To date, Norman has written dozens of books about Clifford and they have been translated into more than thirteen languages.

Pencil trace for the cover of
Clifford the Big Red Dog, Circa 1963

FANS SHOW THEIR LOVE

A painting Norman sent in response to his first piece of fan mail, Circa 1964

Through fan mail, Norman has made many unique connections to his readers. "I always try to answer each fan letter," says Norman. "If a child cares enough to write, they deserve a reply."

Norman's maintained decades-long correspondence with some children (now adults, of course), and he's been contacted by adults who tell him about the meaningful letters they received from him when they were children. Norman even dedicated a book to one fan that he'd never met. "He struck me as being very special," says Norman. "His mother later wrote and told me that the dedication made him feel like a star."

THE BIG RED DOG GETS EVEN BIGGER!

Norman turned his love of art into an astounding accomplishment. In addition to starring in many books, Clifford has been featured in several movies, an animated television series on PBS KIDS, and even in live musicals. "You've just got to press on and keep trying," says Norman. "If you like what you're doing and keep working at it, then someday you will succeed."

"If things go wrong, **DON'T GIVE UP.** Go back and try again."

Art from "Clifford the Big Red Dog"
PBS KIDS television series

TO THE REAL EMILY ELIZABETH

I'm Emily Elizabeth,
and I have a dog.

My dog is a big red dog.

Other kids I know have dogs, too. Some are big dogs.

And some are red dogs.

But I have the biggest, reddest dog on our street.

This is my dog — Clifford.

We have fun together. We play games.

I throw a stick,
and he brings it back to me.

He makes
mistakes sometimes.

We play hide-and-seek.
I'm a good hide-and-seek player.

I can find Clifford, no matter where he hides.

We play camping out, and I don't need a tent.

He can do tricks, too. He can sit up and beg.

Oh, I know he is not perfect.
He has **some** bad habits.

He runs after cars.
He catches some of them.

He runs after cats, too.
We don't go to the zoo anymore.

Clifford loves to chew shoes.

He digs up flowers.

It's not easy to keep Clifford.
He eats and drinks a lot.

His house was a problem, too.

But he's a very good watchdog.

And the bad boys don't come around anymore.

One day I gave Clifford a bath.

And I combed his hair,
and took him to the dog show.

I'd like to say Clifford
won first prize . . .
but he didn't.

I don't care. You can keep all your small dogs.

You can keep all your black, white,
brown, and spotted dogs.

I'll keep Clifford . . . . Wouldn't you?

Clifford
AT THE CIRCUS

FOR JOANNE AND
THOMAS SNEED

I'm Emily Elizabeth, and I have a dog named Clifford.
We saw a sign that said the circus was in town.
A smaller sign said the circus needed help.

We always wanted to join a circus.
We ran there as fast as Clifford could run.

The owner said everything was going wrong.
He didn't think they could put on the show.

I told him Clifford and I would help him. He didn't think a girl and her dog could be of much help.

But I said, "The show must go on."

The first problem was the lions and tigers. They wouldn't obey the animal trainer.

Clifford gave them a command.

They listened to Clifford.

After that the lion tamer didn't worry at all. . . .

Some clowns had quit the circus. The other clowns needed help with their act. I was sure Clifford could help.

Clifford tried on some costumes.

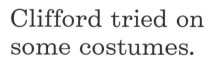

He found one he liked and joined the act.
Clifford enjoyed being a clown.
He wagged his tail. That made the act even better.

The tightrope walker had a sprained ankle.
Clifford tried to walk the tightrope.
He was pretty good.

It wasn't his fault
that he couldn't get
off the ground.

Before the next act we
walked out on the midway.
Clifford loves cotton candy.
He sniffed it.
He sniffed a little too hard.

Licking the cotton candy off his nose made him thirsty. He took a drink. The circus man tried to stop him.

It was too late. Clifford had spoiled the high diver's act.

But he didn't spoil the high diver.
Whew, that was close.

The second half of the circus began
with the elephants on parade.
The biggest elephant had a cold in its nose
and couldn't lead the parade.

So Clifford slipped into an elephant suit
and gave them a hand. I mean a tail.

Then he tried a stunt he thought up.

Oops!

The next act was the human cannonball.
She didn't have any gunpowder for her cannon.
So Clifford helped her out.
He helped her right out of the tent.

Then came the grand finale.
I was going up in a balloon
with the circus man.
Everyone came out to watch.

Oh dear, the rope broke.
I didn't worry.
I knew Clifford would save us.
He rushed to the rescue.

But he missed the rope.
We were blowing away.
Things looked bad.

Clifford didn't give up.
He grabbed an extra tent pole.

He used some telephone wires and took aim.

Bull's-eye!
The balloon was falling like a rock.
We were scared silly.

But Clifford got there in time.
Good old Clifford.

Everybody said it was the most exciting
end a circus ever had.
Clifford saved the show, and me.

Clifford
GETS A JOB

TO BRIDGET MARY,
DEIRDRE, AND
VERA MAURA

Hello—
I'm Emily Elizabeth.

If you don't live on my street,
you may not know me . . .

. . . or my dog, Clifford.

He's a lot of fun to play with.

There is only one bad
thing about Clifford.
He eats a lot of dog food.
And a lot of dog food
costs a lot of money.

We were spending all
our money on dog food.
Mother and Daddy didn't
know what to do.
"We will have to send
Clifford away," they said.

Clifford didn't want
to go away.
He made up his mind
to get a job and pay for
his own dog food.
He decided to join
the circus.
Good old Clifford.

The circus man liked Clifford.
Clifford got the job.

But they put him in the sideshow.
He just sat there. And people just looked at him.
Clifford wanted to do something.

He peeked into a tent.
He saw little dogs doing tricks.
Clifford wanted to do tricks, too.

So he ran into the tent and he tried to jump
through the hoop—just like the little dogs.

It didn't work.

In the next ring Clifford saw
a little dog riding a pony.

Clifford thinks he can do
anything a little dog can do. But he can't.

The circus man was angry.
He asked Clifford to leave.
"Don't worry," I said.
"You can get another job."

So we went to see a farmer.

The farmer thought Clifford would be a good farm dog.
He said Clifford could work for him.

First Clifford rounded up the cows.

Then Clifford brought home a wagon full
of hay. He was doing so well. . . .

And then he saw a rat running to the barn.
Clifford knew that rats on a farm are very bad!

So Clifford chased the rat.

Everything had gone wrong.

Clifford and I started home.
We felt very bad.

Suddenly, a car came speeding past us.

And right behind it came a police car.
They were chasing robbers.

Clifford took a shortcut through the woods —

—and caught the robbers.

I was very proud.
The Chief of Police offered Clifford a job as a police dog.
They don't pay him money. But . . .

. . . every week they send Clifford a lot of dog food.
So now we can keep him. Isn't that wonderful?
Good old Clifford.

Clifford
TAKES A TRIP

TO TRACY

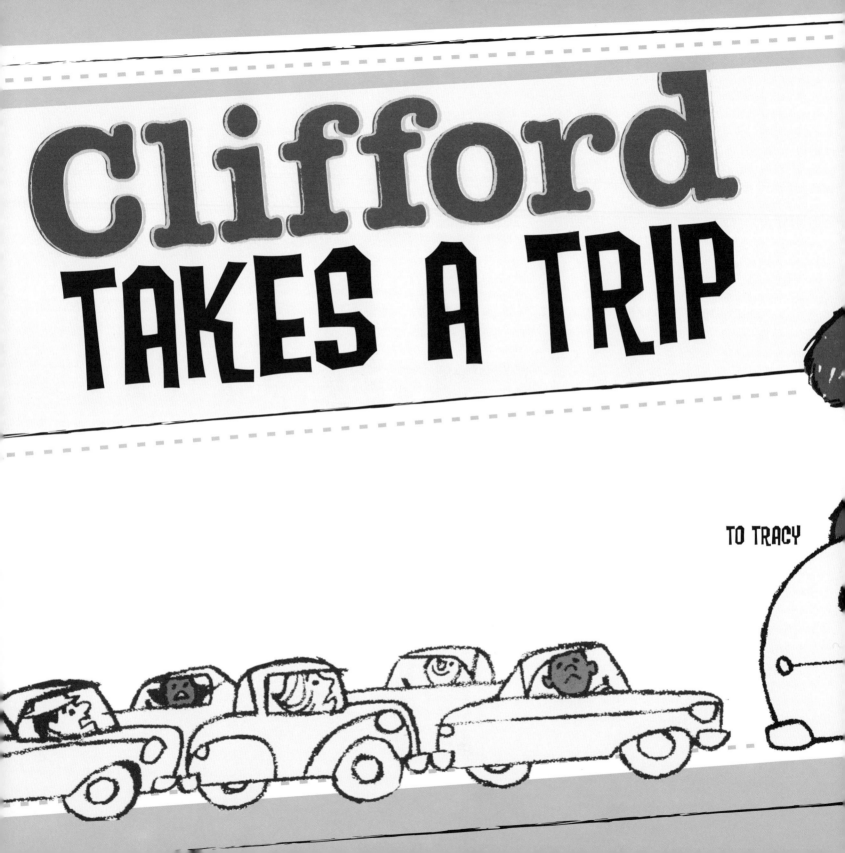

Hi, I'm Emily Elizabeth.
This is a happy day for me.

This is the last day of school.
Summer vacation is here!
Now I can play with my dog, Clifford.

We don't go on long vacation trips.
It's too hard to get Clifford on a bus or train.

We only go to places that Clifford can walk to,
like picnics in the park.

Last year was different.
Last year we went to
the mountains.
Mommy and Daddy
said it was too far
for Clifford to walk.

So we left him with
the lady next door.

That night Clifford
was so lonely...

... he began to howl.
He howled and he howled
and he howled—

—until someone threw a shoe at him.
It didn't hurt Clifford's nose,
but it did hurt his feelings.

The next morning Clifford set out to find us.
He sniffed his way along the road.

Clifford didn't mean to make trouble.
But a lot of people had never seen a big red dog before.

Clifford kept going.
Nothing could stop him.

And then he saw a little old man trying to fix his truck. The man needed help.

So Clifford stopped and helped him. He took the little old man to a garage.

The little old man gave Clifford a little lunch,
to thank him for his help.

Then Clifford set out again.
Nothing stopped him—not even wet cement.

And traffic jams didn't stop him.
Clifford just tiptoed over the cars.
And then . . . .

. . . he came to a toll bridge.
Clifford had no money.

But that didn't stop him.

We didn't know Clifford was coming.

I found some new playmates—
two baby bears.

I was having so much fun.
And then Mama Bear came.

Mama Bear didn't want strangers to play
with her babies. She growled.

Then we heard a LOUDER growl.
Guess who was growling!

Mama Bear was surprised.

She even forgot her babies.
I told Clifford that the Mama Bear
was only protecting her children.

Good old Clifford took the baby bears
back to Mama Bear.

Then he took us all back to camp.
Mommy and Daddy were surprised to see Clifford.

I told them how Clifford saved my life.

So they let Clifford stay with us.

Next year, maybe we will find a way
to take Clifford with us when we go on vacation.

Clifford's
GOOD DEEDS

FOR TIM, STEVE, AND PAUL

Hello. I'm Emily Elizabeth.
This is my dog, Clifford.

A boy named Tim lives across the street.

One day Tim said, "I try to do a good deed every day. If I had Clifford I could help a lot of people." I said, "Let's do some good deeds together."

A man was raking leaves. We wanted
to help him put the leaves in his truck.

I didn't know that dry leaves . . .
make Clifford sneeze.

The man said he didn't
need any more help.
We went down the street.

We saw a lady painting
her fence.

We helped her paint.
When we finished she thanked us.

Clifford felt so happy that he wagged his tail. That was a mistake.

We said we would paint her house, too. The lady said, "Never mind."

Then we saw an old lady
trying to get her kitten down from a tree.
Tim said, "Clifford, get the kitty."

Clifford bent the limb down so the lady could reach her kitten.

But his paw slipped.

Clifford moves pretty fast for a big dog.

The lady was glad to get her kitten back.
It didn't take us long to find our next good deed to do.

Somebody had let the air out of the tires of a car. The man asked if we could help him.

Tim took a rubber tube out of the car and stuck it on the tire valve. Then he told Clifford to blow air through the tube.

Clifford blew.
But he blew a little too hard.

The man felt better when we took his car to a garage.

We saw a small paperboy.
He was so small that he
couldn't throw the newspapers
to the doorsteps.

Clifford gave him a hand.
I mean a paw.

Clifford was a little too strong.

Nothing seemed to go right for us.
All our good deeds were turning out wrong.

Then we saw a terrible thing.
A man was hurt and lying in the street.
Nobody was helping him.

Tim said, "You should never move an injured person." Clifford didn't hear him. He picked the man up. We started off to find a doctor. Oh dear.

We helped the men get their cable back down the manhole. Tim said, "Clifford, maybe you shouldn't help me anymore."

The house on the corner was on fire. Tim ran to the alarm box to call the fire department.

Clifford ran to the burning house. There were
two kids upstairs. With Clifford's help . . .
we got them out safely.

Luckily, there was a swimming pool in the yard.

Clifford put out the fire just as the
firemen were arriving.

The firemen finished the job and
thanked us for our help.

That afternoon the mayor gave us each a
medal for our good deeds.

Of course, Clifford got the biggest medal of all.

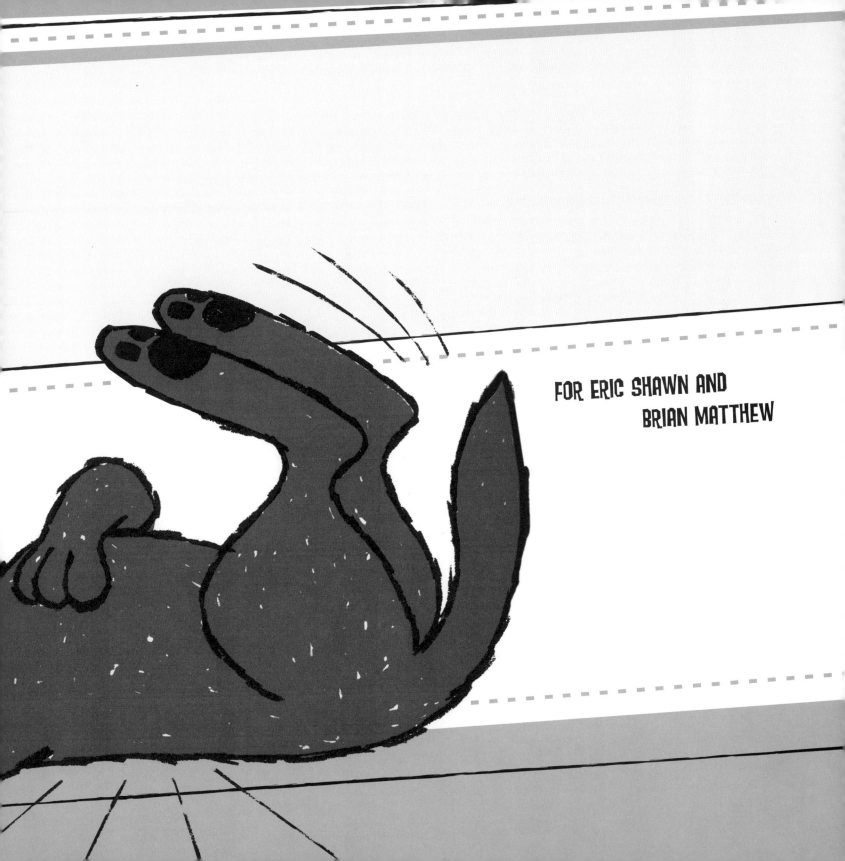

FOR ERIC SHAWN AND
BRIAN MATTHEW

Whee! A new family moved in next door.
They have a girl, and the girl has a dog.

The girl said, "Hi, I'm Martha, and this is my dog, Bruno. He's a very big dog."

I said, "I'm Emily Elizabeth.
This is my dog, Clifford. He's big, too."

"Well," Martha said, "your dog may be a little bigger than Bruno, but I bet Bruno is smarter. I will show you some tricks."

Then Martha sent Bruno to the newspaper stand to bring her a paper.

So I sent Clifford to bring ME a paper.

Martha said, "Bruno plays dead better than any dog I know." He was pretty good.

But not as good as Clifford.
I said, "Clifford, play dead."

Martha said, "Speak, Bruno."
Bruno spoke.

I hated to do it, but I couldn't let Clifford lose.
I said, "Speak, Clifford."

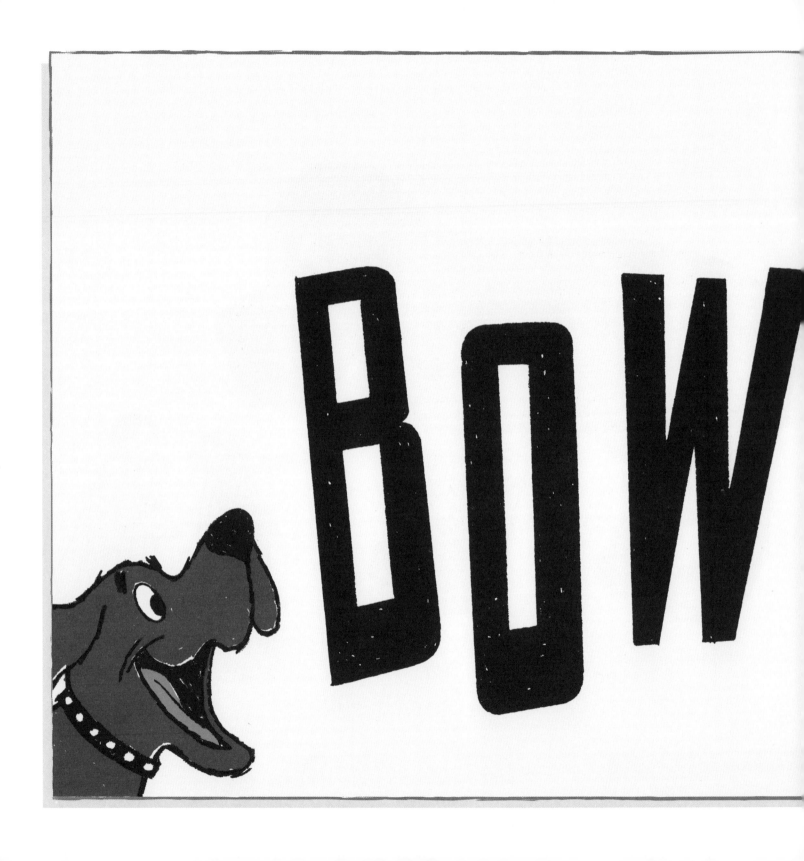

Some people make such a fuss over a little bark.

I told the policemen I wouldn't
let Clifford bark again.
I told them it was just a trick.
They wanted to see Clifford
do another trick.

So I told him to roll over.

That was a mistake.

We decided to take a walk while the policemen talked to Daddy about the car.

Martha said,
"Maybe Clifford is a little bigger and a little smarter, but I bet Bruno is braver."

We walked to the bridge.
"I'll show you how brave
Bruno is," Martha said.
She told Bruno to jump
on the railing and walk.
He was too smart.
He wouldn't do it.

Then Martha did a foolish
thing. She got up on the
railing to show Bruno
how easy it was.

But she slipped.

Bruno was brave. He jumped in to save her.

But he just wasn't big enough or strong enough.
HELP! HELP! HELP!

It was Clifford. Hooray!

The policemen were so happy that they forgave Clifford for mashing their car.

Martha said,
"Thank you, Clifford.
You are the biggest, bravest,
smartest dog I know."

"Thank you for saving
Bruno, because I love him
more than any other dog
in the world," said Martha.

I love YOU more than
any other dog in the world.

Now we both know who is the best dog of all.